LIBRARY OF CONGRESS CATALOGING-IN-PUBLICATION DATA

Katz, Bobbi.   A family Hanukkah / Bobbi Katz ; illustrated by
Caryl Herzfeld.   p.   cm.
Summary: Rachel and Jonathan join their aunts, uncles, and cousins at their
grandparents' house for a traditional celebration of Hanukkah.
ISBN 0-679-83240-8 (trade)
[1. Hanukkah—Fiction.]   I. Herzfeld, Caryl, ill.   II. Title.
PZ7.K157Fam 1992   [E]—dc20   91-51093

Manufactured in the United States of America

10   9   8   7   6   5   4   3   2

A FAMILY HANUKKAH

written by BOBBI KATZ

illustrated by CARYL HERZFELD

RANDOM HOUSE NEW YORK

THE DAYS were growing shorter and shorter. The time for Hanukkah was growing closer. Jonathan and Rachel could hardly wait! Of all the Jewish holidays, Hanukkah was the most fun. There were eight days of festivities—special songs, presents, games, and food. And each day another new candle was added to the family menorah!

THE WHOLE family always celebrated the first night of Hanukkah at Grandma and Grandpa's big old house.

With so many relatives, it wasn't easy to find presents for everyone.

"Let's make a list," said Rachel.

"It's like a game to think of something little and nice—something each person will like," said Jonathan.

THE NEXT day Rachel and Jonathan went shopping. They found some neat things they could afford—a plastic fish for fisherman Grandpa, flower seeds for Aunt Liz and Uncle Bob, a bookmark for Dad and a nifty pincushion for Mom.

But there were other things on their list that cost more than they had expected.

SO THEY started making
gifts—chocolate molds on
sticks and masks for their
cousins, and a beanbag
bunny for the baby.

By pressing cloves into an
orange, they made a spicy-
smelling pomander for
Grandma to hang in her
closet on a ribbon.

AT LAST the day came that would end with the beginning of Hanukkah! Dressed in their best, the kids and their parents piled into the car for the ride to Grandma and Grandpa's house in the country.

THE COUNTRYSIDE looked faded and
frozen under a pale sky. But inside the car,
spirits were warm and bright.

AS SOON as the car pulled into the driveway, the relatives scrambled out of the house to welcome the new arrivals.

After giving hugs and kisses to the grownups, all of the children—except the baby, who was tucked in for a nap—went for a walk in the park with Grandpa.

"HOW COME all you kids are visiting us today?" teased Grandpa as they tramped through a carpet of crunchy brown leaves.

"Oh, Gramps, it's Hanukkah!" said Molly, the littlest cousin.

"'Hanukkah'?" asked Grandpa, pretending to be puzzled. "What's 'Hanukkah'?"

"The Festival of Lights," answered Jonathan, playing along with him. "We celebrate Hanukkah because of a miracle that happened long, long ago in Jerusalem."

"Come on, Gramps. Tell us about it!" begged Molly's sister, Lisa.

"Well," said Grandpa. "It was like this…"

THE MIGHTY Syrian army had conquered little Judea. Their king, Antiochus, had ordered idols of Greek gods to be placed in the Holy Temple.

The Jews refused to worship the statues, but there was no way they could stop the Syrian soldiers from taking over the Temple and sacrificing pigs and chickens to their idols. Meanwhile, the Jews were forbidden to worship God *anywhere*. The punishment for disobeying was…death!

"THEN WHAT happened?" asked Jonathan.
Grandpa continued...

A man called Mattathias and his five strong sons formed a rebel band—the Maccabees. The word *maccabee* means "hammer" in Hebrew. The Maccabees hid in caves by day and struck at night. Shepherds, farmers, craftsmen, and shopkeepers slipped away to join them.

"Put an end to those Maccabees!" ordered King Antiochus.

A huge Syrian army with horsemen and elephants massed in the valley below Jerusalem. But the hammer struck first! The army—elephants and all—was driven away in defeat.

THE HAPPY people rushed to their Temple. They threw away the statues, chased out the animals, and scrubbed the blood from the altar. But when it was time to rededicate the Temple to God by lighting the ever-burning light, they could find only one little jug of sacred olive oil—just enough for one day.

It would take the priests a whole week to prepare a new supply. Yet somehow the ever-burning light kept on burning—day after day for eight days until the new sacred oil was ready! A miracle!

"...AND JEWISH families like ours have been celebrating that *nes gadol*—that great miracle—ever since," added Grandpa. "*Nes gadol hayah sham*—a great miracle happened there. The first letter of each word is on your dreidels."

"I can't wait to play!" said Molly.

"You won't have to wait long," said Grandpa, looking at the sky. "It's almost time to light the candles. Let's go."

THE HOUSE smelled like a cinammon-apple-onion bouquet! While each of the visiting relatives had brought a part of the meal, Grandma herself always made the traditional Hanukkah foods—pot roast, apple sauce, and latkes. Latkes are crispy potato pancakes. And Grandma's were perfect!

AT SUNSET everyone joined Grandpa in singing the prayer as he lit the shammes, or caretaker candle, and then used it to light the first candle in the menorah. Baby Emma banged her spoon with joy as the family sang "Rock of Ages."

Next the delicious meal began. The latkes kept
disappearing, but Grandma piled more and more on
the platter.

"I can't eat another bite," said Rachel. And neither
could anyone else.

AS SOON as the table was cleared, it was time to exchange presents. There were lots of little surprises, but all the kids were most delighted by something that was not a surprise—Hanukkah *gelt*. The chocolate "money" wrapped in gold foil is a reminder of the days when Jews were not allowed to worship God.

Supposedly, they fooled the Syrians by gathering in small groups and pretending to gamble by tossing some coins on the ground and spinning a top called a dreidel.

"IS IT TIME to spin the dreidel?" asked Molly.
A chorus of "Yes! Yes! Yes!" was the answer.
        Everyone took nuts from a big bowl.
        Around and around spun the dreidel as
each person took a turn—winning, losing, or
keeping—according to how the dreidel landed.
Before long, a very happy—and very tired—
Molly had a big pile of nuts in front of her.

THE CANDLES in the menorah burned lower as the family wished each other a happy holiday and left for their own homes.

The first night of Hanukkah was ending, but there were
seven more days to come!

Each night another candle would be added to
the menorah...

until eight candles burned in one bright row,
with the shammes burning above it.